Reconstruction
After the Civil War

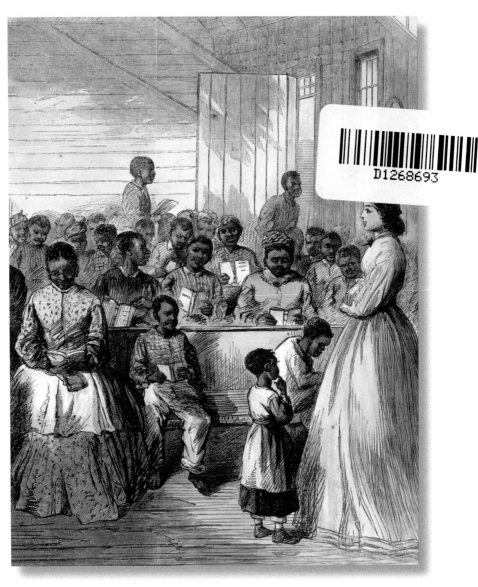

Kathleen E. Bradley

Associate Editor
Torrey Maloof

Editor
Wendy Conklin, M.A.

Editorial Director
Dona Herweck Rice

Editor-in-Chief
Sharon Coan, M.S.Ed.

Editorial Manager
Gisela Lee, M.A.

Creative Director
Lee Aucoin

Illustration Manager/Designer
Timothy J. Bradley

Cover Designer
Lesley Palmer

Cover Art
The Granger Collection, New York
The Library of Congress

Publisher
Rachelle Cracchiolo, M.S.Ed.

Teacher Created Materials
5301 Oceanus Drive
Huntington Beach, CA 92649-1030
http://www.tcmpub.com
ISBN 978-1-4333-0547-4
© 2010 Teacher Created Materials, Inc.

Reconstruction: After the Civil War

Story Summary

After the Civil War, the Southern states were in disarray. Former slaves were now free, but had no homes, money, or education. Uncle Joe, Patsy Berry, and her two children, Moses and Salpy, are working as farmers. The family is waiting for the discharge of Mr. Berry from the military so that they can start a new life together. They receive a letter from Mr. Berry.

The family goes to the local schoolhouse, where the teacher, Miss Kit, reads the letter for them. The letter states that his military service has been extended. Patsy is devastated but is determined to have her family succeed. After an encounter with a carpetbagger, she teaches her children the value of education, and the three of them attend school together.

Years later, Moses and Salpy are adults. Moses is now a teacher, and he uses his father's letter to teach his students about Reconstruction.

Tips for Performing Reader's Theater

Adapted from Aaron Shepard

- Don't let your script hide your face. If you can't see the audience, your script is too high.

- Look up often when you speak. Don't just look at your script.

- Talk slowly so the audience knows what you are saying.

- Talk loudly so everyone can hear you.

- Talk with feelings. If the character is sad, let your voice be sad. If the character is surprised, let your voice be surprised.

- Stand up straight. Keep your hands and feet still.

- Remember that even when you are not talking, you are still your character.

Tips for Performing
Reader's Theater *(cont.)*

- If the audience laughs, wait for them to stop before you speak again.

- If someone in the audience talks, don't pay attention.

- If someone walks into the room, don't pay attention.

- If you make a mistake, pretend it was right.

- If you drop something, try to leave it where it is until the audience is looking somewhere else.

- If a reader forgets to read his or her part, see if you can read the part instead, make something up, or just skip over it. Don't whisper to the reader!

Reconstruction:
After the Civil War

Characters

Uncle Joe	Salpy
Patsy	Miss Kit
Moses	Carpetbagger

Setting

This reader's theater begins on a farm, where
Patsy, her son Moses, and her uncle are working
hard in the hot sun. The setting then changes to
a schoolhouse in town, which was once a hospital
for Confederate soldiers. The scene moves outside
the schoolhouse as a carpetbagger tries to deceive
the crowd with his promises of land. The reader's
theater concludes years later at a university where
Patsy's son, Moses, is the teacher.

Act I

Uncle Joe:	I can tell that the kids are really missing their papa lately. We all do. When will Hiram be discharged from the military?
Moses:	Yes, Mama, when will Papa be coming home from the Rio Grande in Texas?
Patsy:	I'm not sure. Until Hiram comes home, how can we hope for a better life?
Uncle Joe:	Mind the shovel, Moses. There is no need to drift off into one of your daydreams.
Patsy:	Here, son, chew on a fresh green bean. I just picked it.
Moses:	I was just thinking that Papa should be here with us. He should be here to help us farm Uncle Joe's land and work in his garden.
Patsy:	Hush now, child.
Moses:	There is no need to hush, Mama. No one can hurt us anymore for saying what we think.

Patsy:	Well, that might be so, but you never can tell who is listening.
Uncle Joe:	Your mama's right. It is best to be forever mindful.
Moses:	The war is over. I don't understand why the government needs my papa. Why should he guard land on the other side of our country?
Uncle Joe:	Many people feel the way you do, Moses. People wonder why the Texas folk can't guard their own land.
Moses:	Papa fought battles right here in Richmond and Petersburg. He protected the land where he was born. He should be rewarded for that. He should get to come home. He should get to keep some of the land, too.
Uncle Joe:	Moses, lower your voice, son.
Patsy:	Land for us? Right now, be thankful we can help Uncle Joe, rather than a master, build a farm. Once your papa returns home, perhaps we will get a piece of land to call our own.

Moses: But why must we wait? On the way to school the other day, I heard a man talking on a stage. There were flags all around him. He was dressed in very nice clothes. He said that the government will give us a piece of land now that the war is over.

Uncle Joe: I've heard that kind of talk, but I have not seen any land in this state of Virginia being given out for free. General Grant did not get Richmond easily, and neither will we. There will be a price.

Patsy: That's for sure. All of this land was abandoned by Confederate owners and still needs the taxes paid on it. But, who among us has money to pay those taxes when we have been slaves all our lives?

Moses: Uncle Joe, how did you get this land?

Uncle Joe: Well, honestly, the farm isn't mine yet.

Patsy: Uncle Joe has been put in charge of tending it. Until all of the details are worked out, we'll just have to hope that it will be his someday.

Moses:	If Uncle Joe was given some land to tend, why don't we have our own piece, too?
Patsy:	Child, the land will be given to the menfolk, not to a woman like me or to children like you and Salpy.
Uncle Joe:	So until your father is discharged from the First United States Cavalry, you must wait and be patient.
Moses:	Or miss out if he does not return soon.
Uncle Joe:	It looks like we are just about finished picking these green beans. Good timing, too. The sun is just beginning to set. Is that Salpy running down the road? Look at all that dust she is kicking up! She is waving something.
Patsy:	What's that child up to now?
Moses:	It looks like she has a letter.
Salpy:	Mama, it's from Papa! I passed by the postman when I was walking down the road, and he handed it to me.

Uncle Joe: If only we could read it. Open it up anyway, Patsy.

Patsy: It feels like good news. Yes, it sure does.

Salpy: Oh, Mama, I was just dying to open the letter myself on the way home. I wanted to try to read the words. But, Miss Kit says that's not proper. I should only read letters addressed to me.

Uncle Joe: It looks like there is a red three-cent stamp on the envelope.

Salpy: See, Mama, that is your name on the envelope. Papa wrote the letter to you.

Moses: Do you think Papa is telling us that he's finally coming home, Mama?

Patsy: Let's pray that it is so. It has been months since the war ended, and with winter approaching, we need your father now more than ever.

Salpy: There is only one way to find out. Quick! Let's go find Miss Kit. She can help us read it. Then every word will be read just right.

| Patsy: | It won't take us too long to walk into town. I am sure Miss Kit won't mind reading this for us. Let's go. |

Act 2

| Uncle Joe: | Children, not too long ago this schoolhouse was once a hospital for Confederate soldiers. Now, within these same walls, black children receive the education that the Confederate soldiers fought to prevent. |

| Patsy: | It is amazing how quickly things change. |

| Moses: | I can see Miss Kit through the window. She is writing names on the blackboard. Let's go in. |

| Salpy: | Excuse me, Miss Kit, we need your help. |

| Miss Kit: | Why, hello, children! What a pleasant surprise. |

| Salpy: | Miss Kit, this is my mama, Patsy Berry and my uncle, Joe. You already know Moses. He sits by the window over there and giggles all day with the other boys. |

Uncle Joe: Oh, now, Salpy. Mind your manners.

Salpy: It's true. He can't deny it! The other day there was something interesting outside the classroom window. There was so much giggling.

Moses: Please ignore my sister, Miss Kit. She is pretending to know everything again.

Miss Kit: What a nice surprise that you came to visit me. I am just writing our class roster on the blackboard for tomorrow's lesson. See? There are your names. I hope you will come.

Moses: Yes, Miss Kit. We plan to be here.

Miss Kit: Hello, Uncle Joe. Mrs. Berry, it is a pleasure to meet you. Your children are two of my most promising students.

Patsy: Thank you, Miss Kit.

Uncle Joe: I hear her saying to her children every day, "Salpy, Moses, you be mindful when you are at school." Listen to your mother, children, because she is a very wise woman.

Miss Kit:	I want you to know that you are welcome to come to school, too. There are plenty of parents who sit by their children and who learn to read and write along with them.
Patsy:	Before today, I had never set foot inside a schoolhouse. If I had been caught even listening to his children's teacher, my master would have whipped me senseless.
Miss Kit:	Well, there is no reason not to now. That is why the Freedmen's Bureau set up this schoolhouse and many more just like it across the South. You are a free woman, and you are welcome to come learn with everyone else. Here, have a seat on one of these benches.
Salpy:	Miss Kit, we have come to see you because we received a letter from Papa. Can you please read it to us?
Miss Kit:	Certainly. I am pleased to help you. But you and your brother are both learning quickly. I want both of you to try to read along with me.
Patsy:	Here's the letter.

Miss Kit:	Now, where are my glasses? Oh, here they are. This is what your husband writes.
	"Dear Wife, I hope you are well when you receive this letter and that there is no sickness in the family. I miss you terribly, and of course, I miss Moses and Salpy, too."
Patsy:	He is a good man, my Hiram.
Miss Kit:	"I regret to tell you, however, that I have been denied furlough yet again."
Patsy:	Oh, no! That is terrible news.
Uncle Joe:	Now, Patsy, don't worry. Everything is going to be all right. Let's listen to what else he says.
Miss Kit:	"I'm greatly disheartened. I have been sent here to protect the Texas border from the French, who have already seized Mexico. The people in charge tell us that border conditions are still uncertain."
Uncle Joe:	He has already fought in a war between the blue and the gray. Was it not won?

| Miss Kit: | "So, now we must remain in service to protect our country from foreigners. I would rather pay for one year's worth of service and be discharged outright. However, with furloughs refused—unless we pay sixty dollars, which none of us have—we know that a full discharge from the remainder of our service is impossible to purchase. We're trapped!" |

| Salpy: | Please keep reading, Miss Kit. |

| Miss Kit: | "But, my beloved wife, what is even more disheartening is the news that a fellow soldier received today from his wife. She tells him that many of the government's promises made to soldiers' families have been broken. Since the war has ended, rations for her family have been cut in half, and her children are hungry four days out of ten! Do you suffer the same? My heart aches with worry until I hear from you. Your loving husband forever, Hiram." |

Poem: An Army Corps on the March

Moses: Mama, what does it all mean? Why does Papa have to buy his way out of the cavalry? I saw many soldiers return home months ago. Did they buy their way out, too?

Uncle Joe: Here, here. Don't cry, Patsy.

Patsy: No, Moses. Those soldiers joined their units early in the war, so they got released from their service first. Your papa's unit was not formed until two years after the first shot was fired. I suppose that his unit will be kept in service for an equal amount of time and that it will be tacked on to the end of the war. Maybe a fresh start was too much to hope for after all.

Salpy: He'll come home soon, Mama. Don't cry.

Patsy: You're right, child. There is no harm in hoping. That's all we have right now.

Uncle Joe: Thank you, Miss Kit. It's dark outside, and we need to head home now.

Miss Kit: I will walk you outside.

Act 3

Carpetbagger: Forty acres and a mule! That is right, ladies and gentlemen. If you are a freedman, land might very well be yours for the taking.

Uncle Joe: Who is this man standing before that small crowd? It looks as if they have set up a stage just for him.

Moses: Mama, Uncle Joe, that is the man I told you about. He was outside talking to a crowd. Come listen to what he has to say.

Carpetbagger: Who among you is a freedman?

Uncle Joe: Look at them raise their hands.

Carpetbagger: Well, of course you all are. After this war, every man is a freedman, so step up to the stage, fine gentlemen. Clear the way, women and children. There is serious business to be done by the freedmen of this prosperous town.

Miss Kit: Nothing but a carpetbagger!

Salpy: What's a carpetbagger?

Miss Kit: A carpetbagger is a Northerner who moves to the South to take advantage of freedmen. A man like that gives people from the North a bad name! And, he is definitely not from the Freedmen's Bureau, that's for sure.

Salpy: Why would you say that, Miss Kit?

Miss Kit: My brother is an agent with the Freedmen's Bureau, and he does not do business at sundown on a stage in the middle of town. This man is nothing but a showman.

Carpetbagger: Now, today is your lucky day. But by the looks of that sun setting over there, it is nearly over. So, we must be quick about our business.

Miss Kit: What is your name, sir?

Carpetbagger: My name is John Scott and I have purchased a sizable plantation not far from here. As a planter, I am looking to divide the land into 20-acre plots. You heard me correctly! I said 20 acres, folks.

Patsy: This is the kind of deal I have been hoping for.

Carpetbagger: As the planter, I will supply the land for you to tend. I will supply you the tools and the mules that you will need. I will even provide you a cabin to rest your heads after a busy day in the beautiful fields.

Uncle Joe: What do you want in return?

Carpetbagger: I only ask that at the end of one year you give me a reasonable rent plus one half of that fine crop you will be harvesting. A simple plan that is fair, don't you think?

Miss Kit: Do you plan to enter into a formal contract with these men?

Uncle Joe: I would like a contract. Wouldn't the rest of you? Miss Kit, can you oversee this contract?

Carpetbagger: You want a contract? Of course you do, because you are shrewd businessmen. Well, I believe I just happen to have a contract of sorts right here in my carpetbag.

Moses: What is he getting out of that suitcase, Mama?

Patsy: It looks like some papers. It must be his contract.

Carpetbagger: Yes. I have a contract right here just waiting for your signatures. A simple X will do if you have not learned how to write your full name. Never fear—I, John Scott, will add your name right next to your X.

Miss Kit: Gentlemen, do you need my assistance in reading this contract before you sign it?

Uncle Joe: I believe I can speak for all the freedmen here. We would like you to read this contract for us. Here, Miss Kit, take my copy.

Carpetbagger: Miss Kit, that's not really necessary.

Miss Kit: Let's see. Just as I thought. There is no provision here for your families, and you will be hired as gang laborers.

Carpetbagger: Miss, you might wish to go back inside that pretty little schoolhouse of yours and tend to your own affairs.

Miss Kit: Sir, can you guarantee that their day will not be presided over by a man on horseback carrying a whip?

Uncle Joe: Good question, Miss Kit. How do we know this won't be like slavery?

Carpetbagger: Well, now those details have not been worked out completely.

Miss Kit: And can you guarantee them that, at the end of one year, the land will be theirs to own?

Carpetbagger: Not so fast, Miss. You have got to study these things. My word! One might conjecture that you are some kind of lawyer, but we all know that cannot be true. Now, let me see if that note is in there.

Miss Kit: Or, are the terms of this contract so carefully written in your favor that they will have toiled long and hard with nothing to own in the end?

Carpetbagger: Sometimes there are expenses and fees—things of that nature that might not be apparent at first.

Miss Kit: Well then, I suggest you step down from that stage, sir, mount that flea-bitten horse of yours, and head out of town as quickly as you came into it.

Uncle Joe: Patsy, he knows Miss Kit is right. Look at him stuffing that contract back into his carpetbag. He can't get on his horse quick enough.

Salpy: Where is he running off to, Uncle Joe?

Uncle Joe: He is probably riding off to the next town where he can trick someone else into signing his contract.

Miss Kit: We are living in such terrible times that it can be difficult to know who is telling the truth and who is telling a lie. Let's go back inside the schoolhouse to talk. We can light some candles in there.

Patsy: Here, Salpy and Moses. Take the letter and try to read it again. On your own now, focus your minds on it and see what you know. I am going to study this envelope for just a little longer. I am adding my name to the blackboard because I am going to learn to read, too.

Uncle Joe: Salpy and Moses, we have to be careful during this time of Reconstruction. There are people wishing that we will not make it out here in this world of freed people, and we have to prove them wrong.

Patsy: That is why Miss Kit is here. In the end, it is not going to be about how much land we have.

Uncle Joe: It will not be about how many crops we are able to harvest. A fire or a storm could take away both in just the blink of an eye.

Patsy: It is going to be about how much education we get because reading and writing are two things that, once we know them, can never be taken away. Mark my words—come tomorrow morning, I'll be sitting right beside you on that schoolhouse bench!

Song: The Battle Cry of Freedom

Act 4

Salpy: Moses, here is the letter you wanted.

Moses: Thank you for bringing it, Salpy.

Salpy: I can't believe this letter is 50 years old now. It seems like just yesterday when we were standing in Miss Kit's classroom listening to her read it to Mama and Uncle Joe.

Moses: I wonder what my classroom of students will think about this letter? It seems almost like a dream that I am here, teaching in a university.

Salpy: It is not just any university, Moses. You have the privilege of teaching Negroes.

Moses: Papa's letter has been used so often that it is almost too fragile to show anymore.

Salpy: It is a piece of history now. Papa's writing will show them that it was not easy after the Civil War. These young people need to see something real. They need to touch it for themselves.

Moses: Say, why don't you have a seat right here in front so that you can jump in at any point during the lesson.

Salpy: I will take a seat, thank you. And you know I have a few things to say about it.

Moses: Students, the lesson for today is the Reconstruction of the South. Please note that we have a special guest in the class. It is my sister, Salpy Berry.

Salpy: Hello, class. Moses and I both lived through the Reconstruction period.

Moses: In the spring of 1865, all the weapons were laid down. The dust cleared. Our Southern states were ruined. Entire cities were burned. Railroad tracks and bridges were destroyed.

Salpy: The government was not prepared to help four million former slaves. It was especially not prepared to do so while putting our country back together again.

Moses: Groups such as the Freedmen's Bureau were created. They helped to distribute lands, form public schoolhouses, and give out food and medical care. Some Negro men got involved with their local and state governments, too. Change seemed likely.

Salpy: However, change did not come easily. Former Confederates were angered by these new plans. Some formerly enslaved people now worked for wages. Others were sharecroppers. This meant less profit for the plantation owners.

Moses: To offset such progress, unjust laws were created. They were called Black Codes. These codes kept many Negroes working in low-level positions. Families had to live in certain areas. In some states, Negroes were not allowed to own or carry weapons without special written permission. This was true for former Negro soldiers, too.

Salpy: Our parents were among the adults who endured these unjust codes. Eventually, Moses and I grew up and dealt with such things, too.

Moses: My father wrote this letter. He fought for our country during the Civil War and was honorably discharged from the First United States Cavalry in February 1866.

Salpy: He returned home a freedman and farmed land not far from this school. My mother worked as a housekeeper. But, my parents wanted more for their children. Moses and I focused on education. We were our parents' "generation of hope."

Moses: I remember the day my mother received this letter from my father. She said that education is the one thing that cannot be taken away from us. Her words made me realize that change was not going to come easily.

Salpy: Mama was right. She was a very wise woman. The families who did receive land from the Freedmen's Bureau found that their land titles were taken away a few years later.

Moses: President Andrew Johnson gave pardons to former Confederates. These pardons gave them back their lands.

Salpy: Eventually, Southern whites took back control of their state governments. They passed laws allowing segregation to prevail in both Northern and Southern states. Those laws are still in effect in this year of 1915.

Moses: Students, change does not always happen as quickly as we want it to. But as I look out at this class today, I take heart. You are the next generation of hope and change. My dear students, with your perseverance, our people will continue to rise above the challenges that our American ancestors endured.

An Army Corps on the March

by Walt Whitman

With its cloud of skirmishers in advance,
With now the sound of a single shot, snapping like a
      whip, and now an irregular volley,
The swarming ranks press on and on, the dense brigades
      press on,
Glittering dimly, toiling under the sun—the
      dust-cover'd men,
In columns rise and fall to the undulations of the ground,
With artillery interspers'd—the wheels rumble, the
      horses sweat,
As the army corps advances.

The Battle Cry of Freedom

by George F. Root, 1862

Yes, we'll rally round the flag, boys, we'll rally once again,
Shouting the battle-cry of Freedom;
We will rally from the hillside, we'll gather from the plain,
Shouting the battle-cry of Freedom.

Chorus:
The Union forever, hurrah, boys, hurrah!
Down with the traitor and up with the star;
While we rally round the flag, boys, rally once again,
Shouting the battle-cry of Freedom.

We are springing to the call of our brothers gone before,
Shouting the battle-cry of Freedom;
And we'll fill the vacant ranks with a million freemen more,
Shouting the battle-cry of Freedom.

Chorus

Glossary

brigades—groups of soldiers consisting of two or more regiments

carpetbagger—a Northerner in the South after the Civil War, usually seeking private gain under the Reconstruction governments; named this because they usually arrived carrying their things in a carpetbag, or suitcase

conjecture—an opinion or a guess

disheartened—to lose spirit or courage

Freedmen's Bureau—a government agency that helped refugees and former slaves after the Civil War

furlough—a leave of absence granted to soldiers

perseverance—steady determination, especially in difficult times

prosperous—having good fortune; successful

roster—a list of people

segregation—the separation of a race, a class, or an ethnic group

sharecroppers—tenant farmers who give a share of the crops raised to the landlord instead of rent

skirmishers—troops who engage in minor fights

vacant—empty or unoccupied

volley—a firing of many weapons at the same time

undulations—wavelike motions